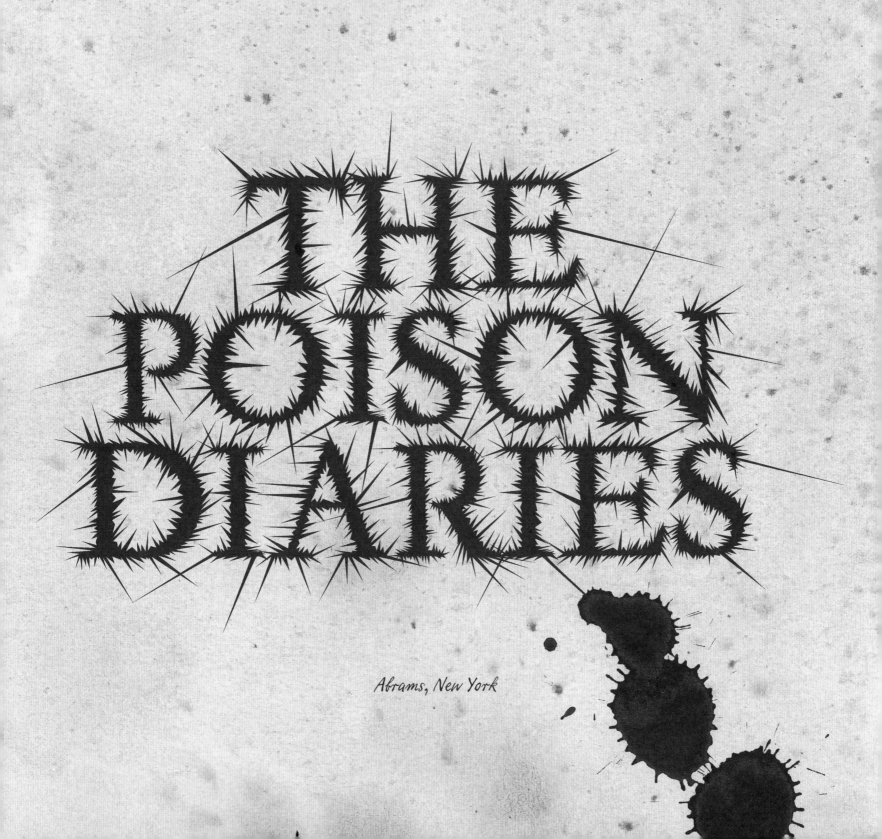

THE POISON DIARIES

Abrams, New York

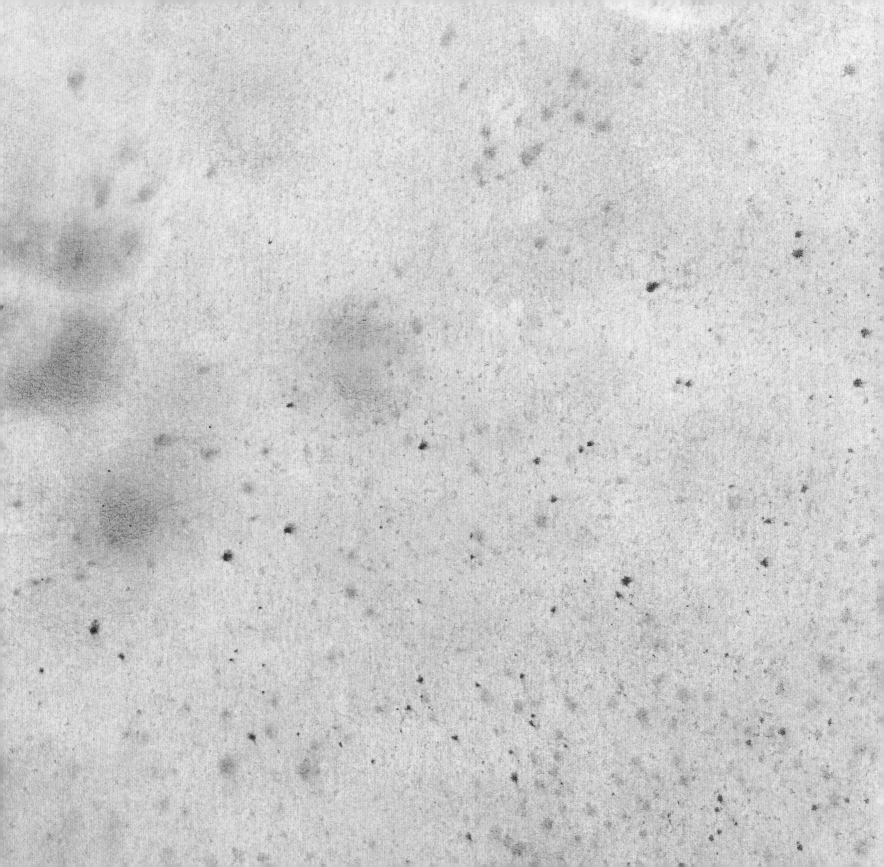

My Journal, by Weed

Today my master, the stinking old apothecary, ordered me to follow him. I obeyed, because I didn't want another whipping, but I still called him a ripe pig fart in my head (the similarity in odour is ever so remarkable).

I ran behind him as he led the way out of the house, into the forest and down the tiny path that leads to the walled place by the ruined monastery. I thought I was the only person who went there, though I have never been able to climb in. People in the village say there are ghosts, and sometimes I have dreamed of arguments and laughter from inside the walls. I would love to see a ghost.

We soon reached the strangely carved gate and to my
delight, the master withdrew a great iron key from the
pocket of his cloak. Turning, he looked at me
with great contempt and spoke thus:
'Weed, you are an unnatural, boy
and a burden on my charity.'
I answered humbly, hoping that he would
finish abusing me and open the gate. Instead,
he cursed me for interrupting him,
then continued.
'Truly, it would have been better
if I had allowed you to die when you
were left on my doorstep.
Nevertheless,
I took you in, and have sought
to give you a trade.'
Trying to appear respectful, I nodded, though in truth
I am more his slave than apprentice.
'Despite the disadvantages of your birth and
a weak mind, you have shown some natural ability
for the apothecary's craft, and it is now
time for you to show your gratitude to me. For I am about to
take you into my confidence. Within these walls lies a garden.
It is no ordinary garden, but contains the most dangerous
poisons known to our trade. The key came into my
possession when I was a young man, and beneath the
soil I found deadly poisons that had lain dormant
here for centuries.

Under my care they flourish once more

'You may touch what you like, for I do not care if you die in agony. However, while you live you shall tend this garden. If you breathe a word of what you do here, then you will die.'

I nodded. With that he placed the key in the lock and turned it. The gate swung open, and peering around the master's stained cloak I had my first glimpse of a very old-fashioned garden.

It was untidy, but there was no foul stench in the air (apart from the master's) and no skeletons, which was a shame, for I like skeletons very much.

I thought I should be disappointed, but instead I had the most peculiar feeling, like a secret part of me was jumping up and down with glee. Here and there were planted shrubs, flowers and a few plants protected within cloches.

The master walked down a path and I followed closely, taking care not to brush against any plants. Eventually, we reached a medium-sized and rather spindly shrub.

'This,' he said, 'is Belladonna. I shall just need a few of the Beautiful Lady's berries for today.

As he bent over the shrub and began to pick its dark, shining berries, a breeze rustled the leaves about us. For a moment I thought I heard a hundred voices, all talking at once, and saying strange things, such as:

'A beautiful boy, is he not? He must be one of ours.'
'He is, of course he is.'
'I'd like to see him chewing on my roots.'
'A child: quick, let us destroy him, haw haw.'

'What?' I asked the master.

'I said nothing, idiot Weed.'

Looking around and seeing
no-one, I feared the master might be right – my mind
is touched. Soon, though, he turned and walked back
towards the gate. While we walked, he talked more
of Belladonna, and for the first time
I listened to him eagerly, forgetting
the voices.

So interesting
were his words that I
resolved to write down
all that he tells me
and draw pictures
of the plants, so that
I may study them
better.
I cannot
wait to see
Marigold
tomorrow
and tell
her
all that
I have
learned.

Plant Properties:

Botanical, Medicinal and Poisonous Uses

Scientific (Latin) Name:
Atropa belladonna.

Other Names: Banewort, Deadly Nightshade, Devil's
Herb, Divale, Dwale, Witch Berries.

Appearance: Belladonna is about two feet to five feet tall with
spreading branches. Its leaves always grow in pairs and one will be
bigger than the other. The flowers are dark violet and the fruit is a
dark shiny black with purple juice.

Symptoms: All parts of the plant are very poisonous, but the roots
slightly more so than the leaves and berries. Just a little Belladonna
will cause a red face and fever, a dry mouth, rapid pulse, dilation of pupils,
headache, difficulty in swallowing, hallucinations, frenzy and convulsions.
If a good doctor is not found quickly, death always follows.

Medicinal Uses: Belladonna can be used as a sedative, to put people to sleep,
and it is also used to make the pupils get bigger for operations on eyes.

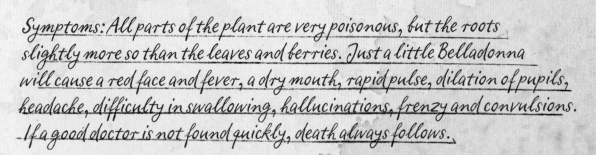

3.

2.

1.

1. Leaves: Paired;
one large, one small.

2. Flowers: Purple
or violet trumpets.

3. Fruits: Dark and
glossy berries with
purple juice and
small black seeds.

4. Stem: Upright
with spreading
branches.

4.

Belladonna

I hear voices carried on the breeze:
they are calling my name again.
The same voices I heard today in the garden.
The same voices as in my dreams.
I am frightened, but I must go to them now.

The garden was dark and quiet when
I unlocked the door. Thinking about the master's
promise to kill me, I turned
to leave, but then a breeze stirred
and at once all the plants began to cry
my name in welcome. Such shouting
and cheering I have never heard.
Some plants, I think they were
Nicotiana, raised their trumpet flowers
and blew a wheezy fanfare, while others
hailed me as The Great Weed.' Dazed,
I walked down the path as if in a dream,
while all around me was noise and joy, until
finally I reached Belladonna.
In a low voice she said, 'Quietly my loves, you confuse the boy',
and the plants fell silent.

I looked down and saw her reaching out to me with her branches
and leaves, and I thought I saw in her flowers and berries the form of
a beautiful woman. Her flowers opened to me and I heard her
voice again, soft and with an accent that I did not know.

'Sit with me a moment, Weed,' Belladonna whispered.

Entranced I fell to my knees. She twisted her stems around me and into my hair.

'Do not fear us, for we have been calling to you for a long time.
All of us here love you and wish to set you free.'

Her flowers nodded gently.

'You will think you are mad, but you are not, you are blessed with
friends such as us all around the world. We will tell you our secrets
and make you powerful.' 'How?'

It seemed that her petals parted in a sweet, sweet smile. With great
satisfaction she said, 'We will make you a master of Life and Death.'

'But I do not want to kill anyone.'

'There have been others like you, and they all said this at first.

But consider that horrible old man
who comes here. We see how he makes you suffer and
for daring to lay his hands on you, he must die. All of us
here are agreed. And after him, together we shall destroy
whoever you please.' 'No!'

My voice shook with terror at the idea of murder.
She drew me a little closer, and her leaves touched my face.

'Let me tell you a story Weed,' she said, and her story was this:

'I once grew in the forgotten corner of a large garden in a country far to the south of here. I heard it called "Italia". In the centre of the garden was a grand house and I would often see a girl laughing among the stupid common flowers.

Roses, I think they were. How I hate roses. All day they talk of bees, bees, nothing but bees. How pleasant it is to watch their empty heads being snipped off and left to die in vases... but I wander from my tale.

'Even though the girl did not come near I could tell she had bright green eyes and twisty black hair like you, and at night I called to her. Sadly, I was alone then and she could not hear, so I waited, knowing she would come sooner or later.

I was quite correct. On a night very like this, when she must have been a few years older than you, she came crawling through some bushes, her gown torn and dirty and her face wet. I was furious to see her made so unhappy and lost no time in offering to help her take vengeance on whoever had upset her so.

'When she saw who spoke she ran away, pulling her hair and screaming that love had sent her mad, but a few nights later she returned, as I knew she must, and told me that the man she loved was to marry her cousin.

'It would have been a great pleasure to make this cousin's next home a lot smaller and underground, if you catch my meaning, and you can be certain that I tried to persuade her, but the girl – her name was *Erbaccia* – would not listen. Instead, I taught her to make herself more beautiful. By letting a drop or two of my precious venom fall into her eyes they became as bright and lovely as stars, so that a man could lose himself in them. Out of love for Erbaccia, I argued that he must be blind, though in truth she had a face that looked as if it had been stung by a swarm of wasps, and the cousin was exceedingly pretty. How we bickered back and forth, but soon time ran out and the day before the wedding little Erbaccia made the only sensible decision and agreed that her pretty cousin must become... how should I say... not so much of a nuisance maybe? A lot less alive, certainly.

'Unfortunately, this still did not win his love.

'Now Erbaccia was already practised at making an essence of my wonderful poison, so it was just a case of making the cousin drink some of it.

Well,
the girl was so trusting of
poor, ugly Erbaccia that this was
easy; a little wine in private
celebration of the marriage and soon,
regrettably, the wedding was off. After all,
few grooms wish their new bride to stagger down
the aisle twitching all over and gibbering from
the pretty visions in her head. Fewer still like to
spend their wedding night watching their beloved's
skin fall off as she breathes her last.'

She must have heard my gasp of horror, for
Belladonna stopped and said sweetly, 'I am deadly,
sweet boy, after all.'

'But what happened to Erbaccia?
Did she get away with it?'

'Oh yes, I am also discreet. When someone drinks my poison they are
rarely able to talk again. The throat swells and the voice is taken away.
No-one found out that Erbaccia had given her cousin a drink that night.'

'And did she get to marry the man she loved?'

'Unfortunately, no. He soon became
betrothed to another famous beauty.'

'So what happened to Erbaccia?'

'Well, she killed that one too of course. And the next. But it couldn't go on. After a few
more deaths on the poor man's other wedding nights, always with the same
symptoms, people began to notice that Erbaccia was always
close by. To escape, she drank my potion herself. I last saw her skipping off
the palace roof in her undergarments. I assume she thought she could fly.
Many do.' 'But if Erbaccia was so unlucky why should I kill anyone?'

'Sweet
boy, poor
Erbaccia lost
her mind
to love.
I tried to help but I could
only do so much. And
besides, Erbaccia only had me.
You have a whole garden of friends to
take care of you.' There were shouts
and cries of agreement. I looked around in gratitude
and noticed it was getting light;
the master would be awake soon.
'I must go now.'
'Very well,' breathed my wonderful new friend.
'But come and see us again tomorrow,
and do think about what we have talked about.'
'I will,' I promised.

Marigold xxx

Last night seemed so real, as if the plants really were my friends, the best friends I ever had (except for Marigold, who is the most beautiful girl in the world).

But I read my journal this morning and it cannot be real. I thought I must be a lunatic. Dear Marigold, she always knows how to make me feel better. When I slipped away and ran to our secret clearing in the forest, she laughed and told me that many people walk in their sleep. Then she kissed me on the cheek. I can still feel her lips there. How I love her and how I wish that I could tell her, but what hope is there for a poor orphan boy who has strange hair and these stupid green eyes. I must never tell her I love her. Never. If she knew, she would want to stop meeting me and I could not bear never to hear her laugh again or watch her smile. After she calmed me, I told her how the master had instructed me on the use of Belladonna

(I can trust Marigold never to tell anyone)

and how the berries could be used to help people when their heart beats too quickly.
Marigold said that
Nanny Gregson suffers like this,
but the village doctor does not know
what to do.

If I one day become a doctor,
perhaps I could even ask
Marigold to marry me.
Tonight I will visit the garden
again, awake this time,
and take more of

Belladonna's berries.

Castor
(aka Ricin)

Scientific (Latin) Name: Ricinus communis

Other Names: Palma Christi, Castor Oil Plant

Appearance: Castor can grow up to twelve feet or more in height and is a tall, but bushy plant with thick, purplish stems and large leaves, which are like hands with seven fingers.
Its poison lies in the seeds, which are pretty and contained in spiky, round pods.

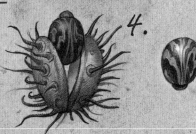

4.

Symptoms: Eating only one seed can kill a grown adult. The first symptom is nausea. After this the victim will suffer violent sickness, stomach pains and diarrhoea.
Then their skin will turn bluey-purple and they will begin to convulse.
Inside, their kidneys, liver, and spleen will all disintegrate, causing death.

Medicinal Uses: Castor oil, which comes from this plant and is treated to remove the poison, can be used as a very strong laxative, but there are no medicinal uses for Ricin.
It can only be used to kill.

1. Leaves: Large and
   divided, like a hand.
2. Flowers: Clustered
   in short spikes.
3. Fruits:
   Soft, spiky pods.
4. Seeds: Three to
   a pod, shiny brown
   and very poisonous.

It is true!

Either I can hear the plants speak or I am a lunatic. As I opened the gate, they shouted their greetings at me again and I almost ran in terror. Somehow, though, my feet found their way to Belladonna and when I knelt she swayed towards me and I felt a flower touch my lips. 'Good evening, sweet boy. I am so glad you have come back,' she said.

'But go and speak to your other friends: learn the secrets that will make you great'.

I pressed my face into her leaves and took some of her berries for Mrs Gregson's medicine, then walked over to the Castor plant, which grew against the opposite wall.

'Hello, Veed,'

he said as I approached. Like Belladonna there was a trace of an accent in his voice. 'Hello, I have heard that you are the most deadly of my new friends.'

'Dead is dead. How big or how small the dose needed is as nothing to the prettiness of the demise, the loveliness of the body in its final throes, the beauty of the thrashing limbs as they try and cling to the last few moments of life, the oh so amusing gasps as they fight for a breath that will not come, the convulsions of the... ahhh spasm! Ah Ah Ah ah Ha HA HA HA HA'!

Castor went stiff and thrashed about, making very strange noises.

'Zorry about that, I become excited you understand. But, yes a speck of the poison that my little babies carry – only a speck – that is enough to take any life.

'Your babies?' I asked.

'Ya,' said Castor with quiet pride. 'Look at my little sweetmeats, zo pretty in their cradles, growing silently until the day when out they spit, free to destroy.'

I noticed that there were lots of spiky pods covering his stems. As I watched there was a **pop** and a tiny seed flew out and hit me on the forehead. Castor giggled.

'Zo zorry, the little ones must haff their fun, no?'

'How are they used? Do you just feed them to people you want to die?'

'Ya, you can do this. But there is a better vay, vould you like me to tell you?'

I was scared, but I nodded anyway. And then he told me this story.

'Not zo long ago I vas discovered by the young man who learned how to make the powder vich kills so vunderfully. He vas a student of science and very cleffer, but he vas also zo poor that he could no longer afford to pay for his studies.

'His name vas **von Rickstein** and his parents vere dead, but his aunt vas rich. If she vere removed... then all the money vould belong to von Rickstein, and he could devote his life to science.

'Von Rickstein had heard about my babies, and vorked night and day in his tiny dark laboratory to discover the secret of their poison, until he had produced a powder vich could kill in zuch tiny amounts that no vun could even see it.

'He named it Ricin. Vunce it vas finished he had to find a vay off giffing it to his aunt. But for a man off his brilliance this vas easy. He read off people many years ago who made pretty rings for the fingers, pretty rings with secrets, ya? Von Rickstein took all of his remaining gold and made vun just the same. On the top vas a beautiful lion. But vun off the claws vas just a little too long, zo that when his happy aunt, who loved trinkets and jewels, put it on, it pricked her finger.

'Inside, the claw vas hollow and contained a few grains of Von Rickstein's new powder. They dropped into the tiny scratch and...
Ahh ha ha HA HA HA

AHHH ha! Spasm, zorry.

'Vithin a few hours the aunt vas finding it difficult to breathe and her skin turned blue. Zoon the ricin was breaking down all the important things inside her body, until it all turned to mush and she died in thrashing agony. Oh it vas magnificent.'

'Vot, I mean what, happened to him?'

'He got the money and became a great scientist. And a great Veed like you could do zo much more. This unhygienic old perzon who claims he is your master could be killed most beautifully, ya?'

'No, no. I don't think I could do that.'

'Ah HA HA he ha ho ho HEE HEEE HEE,'

was Castor's response.

Journal

It was very late when I returned last night, but I distilled a little medicine in the workshop. Then I cleaned the benches and the glass bottles, tubes and contraptions, laid out the alchemy equipment ready for the day, lit the fires and made breakfast. For the master: sausages, bacon, eggs, toast and tea with rum in it. For me: dry toast made with stale bread, and some water.

The master was in a temper when he came down and boxed my ears when the tea burned his tongue. I was too excited to mind very much, thinking about how Marigold would admire me when Nanny Gregson was cured, though I did find myself daydreaming about pouring the bottle of poison into his tea. I am very curious to see what it would do.

But Marigold would never marry a murderer, so I tried to think good thoughts instead. The master worked me harder than ever that morning, but had a large lunch of beer and then retired to bed, so I was able to slip away to the forest. '*Weed!*' Marigold screamed happily when she saw me, and threw her arms around my neck.

I spun her around and we collapsed laughing on the grass. '*Look,*' I said, pulling a small bottle from my pocket when we had finished giggling.

This is for Nanny Gregson. You must mix only the tiniest drop with water each night and then give her only the tiniest drop of that water.'

'Weed, you are so clever. What else can it do?'

'Well, too much
will give you visions of the devil,
but a little in the eyes will make them shine
like stars. I have heard that ladies used
to use it to make themselves irresistible.'
'Really?' said Marigold.
I must go,' I said, kissing her cheek.
Then I ran back to the cottage.
I was too late though; the master was
awake and had a sore head. The
burners had gone out and
his potions were ruined.
Catching me
around
the neck,
he tore off
my shirt and
beat
me.

Lords & Ladies

Scientific (Latin) Name: Arum maculatum

Other Names: Cukoo Pint, Arum, Starchwort, Adder's Root, Friar's Cowl, Kings and Queens, Wake Robin, Quaker.

Appearance: Usually about six inches high (though it can grow up to about two feet), Lords and Ladies has its flowers concealed by a hood-like leaf, which is called a 'spathe', out of which pokes a fleshy stem. Late in the year, the flowers give way to beautiful clusters of bright red berries and the leaves fall off.

Symptoms: Only one drop of berry juice causes a burning in the mouth and throat. If whole berries are eaten, the burning is followed by weakness, vomiting and horrible diarrhoea. Before dying, the victims will also experience intense convulsions.

Medicinal Uses: Lords and Ladies' roots have been used to cure ringworm, but only after they have been stewed for several hours, otherwise the skin blisters. In very, very diluted doses it can help a sore throat.

1. Leaves: Long and veined, sometimes with dark spots.

2. Spathe: Conceals and protects the flower; the goblet at the bottom is a trap for insects.

3. Flower: A brown spike emerges from the goblet, in which are small flowers.

4. Berries: Bright and glossy red.

Tonight

I went straight to see the Lords and Ladies. Belladonna had told me a little about them, so I wore my best rags and had combed my hair so that it looked slightly less twisty than usual. As I approached the small plants I bowed deeply, though my back was covered with cuts and bruises, and said that it was an honour to be in their presence. Then I went down on my knees.

'Indeed, you are fortunate to have benefactors such as we,' said one in the haughty female voice. 'Is it not so my lord?'

Another plant answered gruffly. 'Eh, what's that you say? What's this? Looks like disgustin' vermin to me. Let's kill the blighter. He'll learn some respect for his betters when his life is dribbling out of his backside, haw haw.'

'It is a child, but the special one. You remember: the young person that the common plants have been gossiping about. It wouldn't become us to dispense with him, but still one wonders why he has left it so long to present himself. Was it a deliberate snub do you suppose?' As the lady spoke, I thought I saw her peering down at me over some spectacles on a stick, though even kneeling I was much taller than the plants.

'My Lords, my Ladies,' I said in my most humble voice. 'Everything is so new to me that I fear I have given offence where none was intended. I assure you that I am your most obedient servant.'

The gruff voice spoke again. 'He grovels well, m'dear, haw haw. Perhaps we can do something with the boy, though he is a child.' 'Do you not like children my lord?' 'Pah, children!' he answered.

'Runnin' around all happy and carefree when they should be tremblin' before us. We don't like 'em, we hunt 'em.'

'Let us tell the young man about the fun we had last season, my lord,' chimed in the lady. And together they told me. 'Your common vermin, haw haw, like to trespass in fields and woods that rightfully belong to us, pollutin' the fresh air with their shoutin' and laughin'.'

'I am sure you will agree that such disgracefully criminal behaviour simply cannot be suffered,' the lady continued. 'One has to maintain one's position in society. These pestilential creatures must be taught to respect the superior class.' I didn't agree at all, but thought it would be wise to hold my tongue.

'As I was sayin', we sportsmen lie in wait in the woods and the hedges, usin' our jewels as bait to tempt the vermin. There's not many poor children as can resist sweet and plump red berries. Do you remember that brace we caught last season, m'dear? A boy and a girl, young and tender.'

'Of course I do, my lord. They must have stuffed nearly a hundred into their vulgar, thieving stomachs before the burning started.'

'Haw haw, the burning. They were clawing at their mouths and throats for ages, weren't they m'dear? Didn't even notice they were growin' weaker and weaker?'

idiot creatures. And when they were-

...eeble to run, the entertainment really began. I am a connoisseur, Master Weed, and the convulsing, writhing and groaning of these two children was quite genius, a marvellous display. And the fountains of vomit! Spectacular! It took hours for them to finally perish, but you should have heard the applause when they did. We simply had to hold a ball to celebrate. It was a great success.

I had already heard some dreadful tales of murder in the garden, but this story, so cheerfully told, filled me with disgust. Yet still a part of me was fascinated by these haughty and cruel plant, and I smiled when I thought what the hateful old apothecary would look like convulsing and spurting sick. 'I must say special child or no, a few berries might teach him better manners.' 'Haw haw, m'dear, haw haw haw.'

'My Lords and Ladies, if I may take my leave,' I said as I backed away. 'Well! Kw rude.' I heard as I retreated. And just. Horrified by how tempting this vision was, I rose, as quickly as I dared, and bowed.

Scientific (Latin) Name: Nicotiana tabacum

Other Names: Tobacco, Tabacca

Appearance: Nicotiana has a long, hairy stem that splits near the top into branches and grows from three to six feet high. Its leaves are large, pointed, pale green, and smell strongly, while the flowers are long, trumpet-shaped and usually a pale pink.

Symptoms: Nicotine is a very powerful poison, and can be absorbed into the body through the skin, or into the lungs by smoking the leaves, or it can be eaten. Sickness, dizziness, headache, diarrhoea, and shaking hands are followed by a racing heart and a cold sweat. The victim will then become unconscious and begin to convulse before a heart attack finishes him off.

Medicinal Uses: There are no benefits at all from smoking Nicotiana, but it may be of use in small doses in the treatment of those afflicted with mental illnesses.

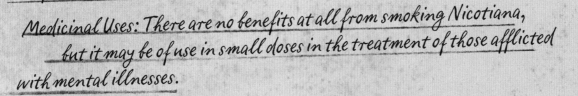

3.

Nicotiana

1. Leaves:
Large, alternate
and light green.

2. Flowers: Long,
pale pink or white
trumpets that swell
slightly at the 'throat'.

3. Fruits: Oval
pods containing
many seeds.

2.

1.

It wasn't difficult to find Nicotiana in the dark: I could hear her coughing from the gate when I let myself into the garden. As I got closer I could smell her heavy, powerful perfume, too. I took a deep lungful and breathed out slowly.

'Howdy handsome, cuuhurggh, huugh. Ain't I smellin' lovely today?' Nicotiana hacked and wheezed at me, and I thought I saw one of the other plants spit out a great lump of brown phlegm.

'Darn, it's great to expectorate,' she rasped.

'Erm, hello Nicotiana,' I said. 'Darlin', curuugh, Nicotiana's too formal 'tween you an me,' she said in a wheedling voice. 'We is gonna be real good friends. See here, I ain't never gonna let ya go and I got lotsa better names friends can call me by. I know: why dontcha call me Madam Baccy? Short for Tobaccy, ya unnerstand?'

'Yes, I think so. Err... Madam Baccy, I was wondering how poisonous you are?' 'Why, how kind o' y'all t' ask. Fact is, I'm killin' hunnerds o' folks every cotton-pickin' day. It's a wonder a gal can keep up with demand.' I was beginning to like Madam Baccy, and her smell was becoming sweeter and sweeter.

'Ya see, t'other pizens here is all good cultivated folks,' she continued, 'but they don't got ay-dic-shun. I'm tellin' you — ay-dic-sun is where it's at.'

Cuh-hoooey cuhurrgh.

Sure, a few people gonna eat a few berries by accident occasionally, an' a few folks me'bee use ya t' kill someone. Shoot, I even gets used that way myself sometimes, an' darn good I am too. But them folks with ay-dic-shun are sure enough lining up at the store to pizen themselves with ole Baccy. Jest imagine that! Thousands of 'em, smokin' them pipes and ceegars and cigarettes til they jest plain pizen themselves t' death. Why dontcha take a seat down there handsome, an' I'll tell ya all about it.'

I sat down next to her and sniffed hard at her flowers. They made me feel ever so slightly sick. 'I'll tell ya the story of a young man name o' Beau, 'bout the same years of age as yourself.

'A prime young 'un he was too. He could run alongside the horses all day long an' lift a cartwheel in each hand. All the young ladies were jest nuts about Beau, an' I could hardly wait t'get my leaves in him neither. Course it din't take long; as he got closer to manhood he saw all the men round him puffin' away and thought if he were t' be a man he better get puffin', too.

'I remember the first time he tried a ceegar. Went as green as a toad and sicked his vittels up, cuuurgh cuh. His heart went a-racin' and he was sweatin' all over. You'd o' thought that he dint want t' do that agin wouldn't ya? But young Beau he was so bent on bein' a man he jest kep' tryin' and tryin', til finally he grew t' like it. By that time the ay-dic-shun had him good. If he didn't have ole Baccy every day, he'd jest get grumpy as a grizzly bear that's sat on a bee. Now the other pizens round here ain't got no patience. They wants t' kill ya good an' quick, but I don't mind takin' it slow. As I always says, pizening folks is like eatin' a good steak: you want t' savour every darn moment.

'So over time Beau started not t' run so quick, an' then he hardly could run at all without spluttering up all sorts of nasty stuff. Coough cuh.

'Kinda like that. Now's the time, I thinks t' myself, t' lay him in his grave. So I invited a pardner o' mine – name o' Cancer back west – into his black ole lungs an' that was the end a' Beau. (Well, after a year o' painful wastin' away.) That's the beauty of ay-dic-shun: folks jest do it to themselves.

'Once ya had a taste o' Madam Baccy, it's kinda difficult t' say goodbye. As I walked back to the gate I could hear her calling to me, 'Ah'll be seein' y'all real soon handsome, coooooyugh, coooourrrgh.

I already wished I could go back.

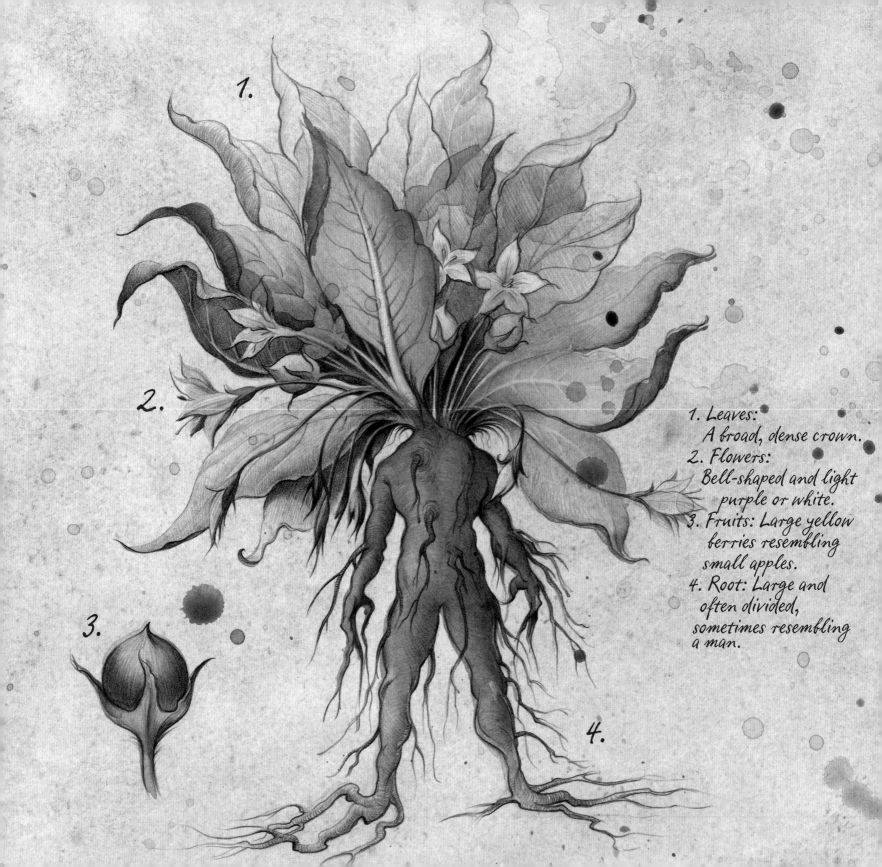

1. Leaves:
   A broad, dense crown.
2. Flowers:
   Bell-shaped and light
   purple or white.
3. Fruits: Large yellow
   berries resembling
   small apples.
4. Root: Large and
   often divided,
   sometimes resembling
   a man.

Scientific (Latin) Name: *Atropa mandragora*

Other Names: Mandragora, Satan's Apple

Appearance: Above the ground a crown of leaves can be seen, each a foot long, five or six inches wide, and dark green. The bell-shaped flowers are usually white, with a tinge of purple. These give way to a round fruit, looking and smelling like a small yellow apple. Below the ground, Mandrake has a long, thick root, which sometimes branches and can look like a human.

Symptoms: Mandrake's poison is similar in action to Belladonna's. Eating any part of the plant will produce nausea, a rapidly beating heart, and madness.

Medicinal Uses: Mandrake was used long ago to make people sleep and to ward off pain during operations. Some people also said that a small dose could ward off demons, perhaps because it can be used to calm maniacs and the mad. The leaves can be used as a cooling poultice for skin complaints.

Mandrake

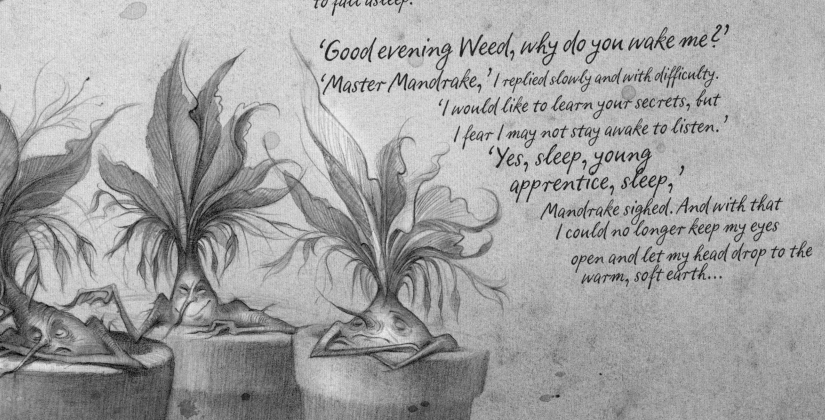

I found Mandrake in a
quiet part of the garden, and just
smelling the leaves that spread out over the
pots where he grew made me feel sleepy. I had to

shout quite loud

to wake him, but finally he stirred and spoke in a curious
deep, drowsy voice that made me feel like that moment
when you are warm in bed and just about
to fall asleep.

'Good evening Weed, why do you wake me?'

'Master Mandrake,' I replied slowly and with difficulty.
'I would like to learn your secrets, but
I fear I may not stay awake to listen.'
'Yes, sleep, young
apprentice, sleep,'
Mandrake sighed. And with that
I could no longer keep my eyes
open and let my head drop to the
warm, soft earth...

Immediately, I began to dream. There stood before me a young man with a floating mass of hair and a long, dark green cloak. He smiled at me, snapped his fingers and I felt time go backwards. Thousands of years whirled round us in an instant and then stopped.

There, shimmering in the heat, was a great city with a beautiful fortress covered with trees and flowers.

'This is Babylon,' said Mandrake in his slow voice. 'We shall visit the first to discover my powers, a young man called Mesilin. You would call him a doctor.' We walked through bustling streets and into the palace.

Mandrake led me down a maze of corridors until we reached a bedchamber. Silks and tapestries hung from the walls and the furniture was inlaid with precious metals and stones. On the bed, a young man lay unconscious and a tall man was bent over him. He was cutting the boy's leg off with a saw.

'The boy on the bed is a prince, the nephew of a great king. His leg was wounded in a hunting accident and it has now become rotten. The only way to save him is to remove it.'

'But what has this to do with you Mandrake?'

'You see how quiet and still the prince is? The doctor recently discovered that a drink prepared from my root will make anyone who drinks it sleep through even the greatest pain. He has given it to the boy.'

'So you help people?' I asked eagerly.

Mandrake considered for a moment before replying.

'Yes, I suppose that could be said, but watch. Mesilin has given the boy too much.'

With that, Mandrake walked over to the boy and, unseen by the doctor or the guards, he placed a hand on the boy's head. 'Yes,' he said quietly. 'That is the way. Go down where it is warm.'

I knew that the prince had died.

Mandrake turned his great head towards me and said, 'You see Weed, unlike your other friends, I am gentle. But I am just as deadly. If you wish to remove this apothecary of yours, I can make it seem that he died peacefully in his sleep.'

As I watched, Mesilin noticed the change in the prince. He held his ear close to the boy's mouth and felt all over his body for signs of life, then he became agitated and ordered the guards out of the room.

He barred the
door and quickly drank
deeply from a jar,
weeping all the time.
'What is he
doing?' I asked.

'He knows that the
king will have him
executed for his
nephew's death.
Mesilin has drunk
his own potion and
will soon fall asleep.
By the time that the door
is broken down and they
drag him away to the dungeon,
he will be dreaming sweetly and will
not know or care.

Then the world started spinning and the
next thing I knew, I was woken by the belt of
my master across my back.

For a moment I thought I was in the garden, but I was in my own bed.
How I had returned I don't know. All I could think of as he lashed me, is how good
it would be to watch him fall asleep, never to open his eyes again.

What have I done?

Oh my love, my beautiful Marigold. I waited for her in our clearing, but she was late. When I was about to leave, she staggered through the trees. She was trying to scream, but her voice wouldn't come. I thought she must be ill and laid her down on the grass. She looked up at me and her eyes were huge and staring and full of madness. I knew then what had happened.

'Weed, Weed, Weeed,' she managed to gasp with great effort, though I could barely hear the words.

'I thought that Belladonna might help make you love me, like I love you.' And she shivered and clung to me.

I began to sob, holding her tight. 'I do love you Marigold. There was no need for poison.'

'Only a little. I only put a little in my eyes.' My tears fell on to her face and I wished I was dying too. She fell silent and her body became still. I put my face next to hers, 'Will you marry me, Marigold?' I asked.

For a second, something flickered in her fixed, wide eyes and she mouthed the word 'Yes'. Then she was gone.

I went home to a beating that I didn't feel. I had only one thought - the plants have killed my love and they must die too.

Marigold is

Henbane & Hemlock

Henbane

Scientific (Latin) Name: Hyoscyamus niger

Other Names: Hog's Bean, Jupiter's Bean, Symphonica, Henbell, Cassilata

Appearance: One to two feet in height, Henbane's stems are covered with long, sharply pointed, hairy oval leaves, each of which has a spike on each side. Flowers grow densely and are yellowish with purple veins. The fat little fruit pods contain about 200 seeds each.

Symptoms: Henbane is sometimes called the 'sleeping herb', but severe poisoning causes hallucinations, impaired sight, and uncontrollable spasms similar to those caused by Belladonna.

Medicinal Uses: In very mild doses, Henbane relieves muscle pain and aids sleep.

Hemlock

Scientific (Latin) Name: Conium maculatum

Other Names: Herb Bennet, Spotted Corobane, Musquash Root, Poison Parsley, Kex

Appearance: Hemlock can grow up to five feet high and has a hollow, round stem with purple spots, from which branch many small leaf stems and sprays of small white flowers.

Symptoms: Burning in the mouth, sickness and diarrhoea, muscle tremors, convulsions and, in severe poisoning, paralysis causing death.

Medicinal Uses: Hemlock has been used as an antidote to strychnine poisoning and as a remedy for cramp. It must be used very carefully.

Henbane
1. Leaves: Sharply pointed.
2. Flowers: Dusty yellow
and veined with purple.
3. Fruits: Seeds are found
within two compartments.

Hemlock
4. Leaves: Bright green;
many smaller leaves grow
from each stalk.
5. Flowers: Clouds
of small white
flowers.
6. Seeds:
Tiny,
oval
and
ridged.

1.

2.

3.

4.

5.

6.

I walked up to Belladonna
with a scythe and told her
coldly what I must do.

'But, sweet boy,' she said, 'I did not kill this girl, I only helped the old woman.'

'If you hadn't told me your stories I would never have told her that she
would be more beautiful with poison in her eyes.'

'Then it is you who are the killer, not I,' replied the lady.

'You should have told her not to touch it. Did I not tell you I am deadly?' I knew that
what she said was the truth. I fell to my knees sobbing.

'Sweet boy, go and see Mistress Henbane.
She will calm you.'

A plant greeted me with a cackling laugh. 'You've found
Henbane dearie; now we shall do some dark magic,
some vile deeds by the light of the moon. Hail
Weed, who shall be king hereafter... O' course you'll
also be wanting the 'elp of me 'usband, the famous Master
'Emlock

'oo pizened the great Socrates.'

'Shut up, you stupid plant. If he wants my
help he will ask for it,' spoke another, rather
taller, plant nearby. 'Blow it out yer stalk, yer silly old geezer.' 'Why you poisonous crone,'

I'll strangle you, I'll...' 'Er, did you say something about me being king?' I interrupted. 'Oh, don't listen to her drivel,'said Hemlock, 'She tells everyone that. But you are upset. Sniff my wife, though she is a stinking old baggage, and be calm.' I put my face into Henbane's leaves and breathed deeply. Soon I felt quiet and not so much like weeping. Hemlock and Henbane watched and then told me a story. 'It was a long time ago', began Hemlock, 'In a village lived a girl called Meghan who was a brilliant witch. Clever she was...' 'And lovely,' continued Henbane. 'Don't forget that, yer dried up old twig. She were a great beauty. All the men wanted to marry 'er. But she refused 'em all and 'elped people instead. She delivered babies, cured sickness and did a little magic for anyone 'oo asked.'

'Anyway,'
broke in Hemlock, 'even in
those days, being called a witch
was asking for trouble. Nevertheless,
her fame spread far and wide and one
day a great lord came to see her for himself.
   Like many before him, he immediately fell in love
with Meghan and was furious when she refused him.
   'Such a man wasn't very 'appy about bein'
sent packin' by a peasant gel. So he decreed she was
a witch an' had 'er tortured. All the while she cried out, but the villagers
was so scared that none o' them lifted a finger to stop the lord's men.
   'When she was bleedin' and half dead, they finally let 'er go and
she went home and set to
work right away,
   making the nastiest
little potions.

'Once she'd finished, she climbed into the
tavern cellar an' pizened all the beer wiv 'Emlock.
Then she poured the bucket of potion she made from me leaves
down the village well.
'That night, the villagers drank their water as usual.
For a while everything was quiet, but then Henbane took hold of them
and it was as if the whole village had turned into demons. People tore off
their clothes and jumped around like fiends, setting fire to their homes and
gibbering.'
'Them in the tavern 'ad been drinking 'Emlock all night, Weed',
Mistress Henbane interrupted. 'When they 'eard the commotion they tried
to go and see what the trouble were, but found they couldn't move. Not a muscle.
When the village people burst into the tavern and danced mad jigs,
there weren't nothing the lord an' 'is men could do but sit and watch
and feel their breath runnin' out.
'After a while Meghan came to join the party. She sat next to the great
lord and told him he was dying, then she
watched the villagers fall into a twitching sleep from which
none would ever wake. By morning, everyone was dead
except Meghan.'
Despite the horror of the tale,
I found myself laughing at the
vengeance Meghan had taken.
As I walked home, I wondered if I
still could be the Great Weed.

A man came from London today and took away a great box of potions my master and I had prepared. The foul-smelling old dung heap thinks I do not know what they will be used for, but the plants have taught me well; every bottle and vial in the box is deadly. My disgusting master sells poison to people who kill. What a fine couple we make — he is a murderer and I am his apprentice killer.

After all, Marigold would still be alive if it were not for me. Men from the village found her body today. No-one knew that we met in the clearing and they are saying that she must've poisoned herself by eating berries that she found in the woods. My master suspects nothing, but thinks I'm truly mad now. Maybe he is even a little afraid of me, for I can distil and refine poisons faster than he can now, and without his instructions. He questions me, but I smile and say nothing.

But Marigold was an accident. I did not murder her and she loved me; she would not want me to kill anyone. I must be good for her sake. No, I am the Great Weed and it will be a joy to watch the master die. I know a lot already: I could make it so painful that he would be glad of death, or so gentle he would not even know I had taken his life. I could be a killer and have all of my friends around me always, or I could be good and be beaten every day and not have a friend in the world. I wish Marigold was here. The plants will know, the plants will help me.

All I think about is death and poison. Perhaps I am becoming one of them now: my toes feel as if they would like to burrow into the earth, my hair is growing more quickly than it should, and in my old, cracked mirror my eyes shine more brightly green than ever. I should be sad, but I am not because I am Weed, I am poison. Marigold is dead and nothing matters. If someone so perfect and so beautiful can suffer and die, then so can everyone else.

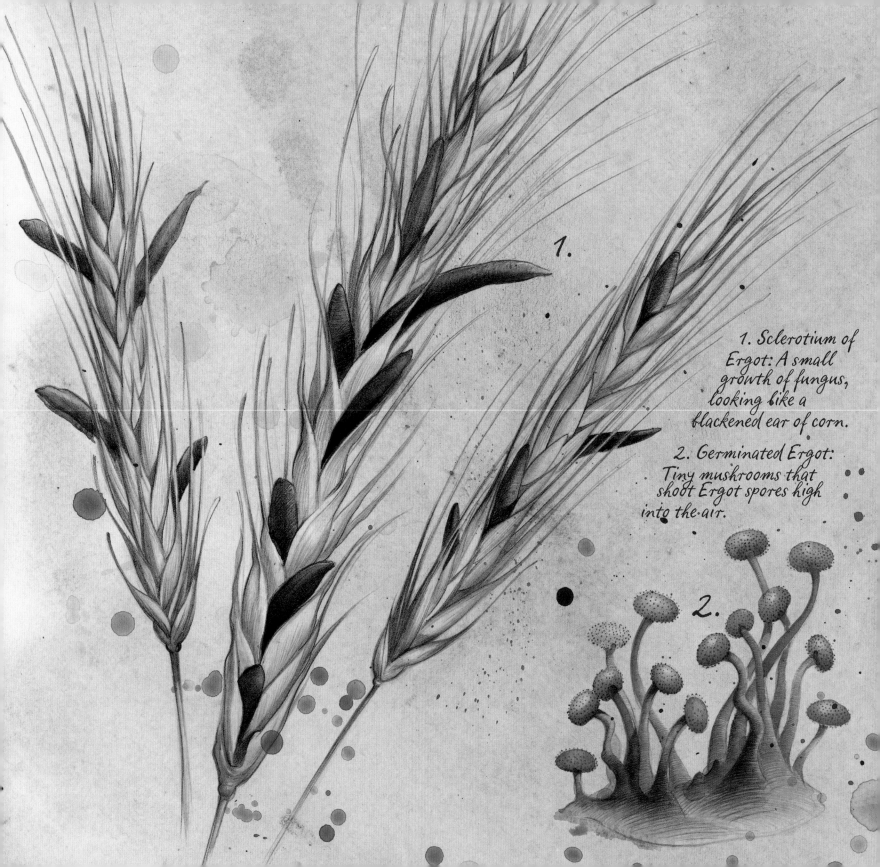

1.

1. Sclerotium of
Ergot: A small
growth of fungus,
looking like a
blackened ear of corn.

2. Germinated Ergot:
Tiny mushrooms that
shoot Ergot spores high
into the air.

2.

Scientific (Latin) Name: Secale cornutum

Other Name: Claviceps

Appearance: Looking like an ear of wheat that has been burned by the sun Ergot is a small, curved fungus that grows on cereals and is easy to miss if not looked for.

Symptoms: Drowsiness, severe stomach pains and vomiting are accompanied by a strange sensation in the fingers and toes as well as dizziness and wide pupils. As the level of poison increases, the victim will suffer convulsions and hallucinations. In some cases, gangrene will wither the limbs.

Medicinal Uses: In the past, small doses of Ergot have been used to calm hysteria and asthma, as well as body tremors.

He had a funny accent too, and I nearly laughed, but I
wanted to hear his story too much.
'I'm sorry
Mr Ergot, truly. I did not wish to suggest
you were anything less than a terrible killer.'

This seemed to calm him a little. 'You
weel address me as Field Marshal
Ergot, or My Lord! Anuzzer word of your
insolence and I weel order my ants to attack.'
'Yes Lord Field Marshal Ergot Sir.'
''Zat ees better; I see you 'ave ze look of a
military man. Well, I shall tell yoo tales of

strategy and war and destruction, of cannon
firing spores into the sky and ze enraged whinnies
of my loyal legions of ants battling to take me where
I can do ze most damage. For Death, for Glory,
for Veectory!' And his tale was this.
'France, some while ago, as yoo living persons say. I was
but one spore in a mushroom zat was not much bigger than
ze 'ead of a pin, but I was destined for greatness. Close by
was a town of ze living. Pah 'ow I 'ate ze living. Walking about as
eef zey own ze place, just because of zeir 'orrible great size... so
clumsy, so inelegant. Above me grew ze wheat zey like to eat so much
and I knew zat if only I could enlist ze 'elp of my bruzzer soldiers
and get an army to ze top, I could cut ze stupid living down to size.
'All zat 'ard winter I toiled, planning tactics and training my ant
troops. I sent word to all ze ozzer beetle mushrooms,
and by spring we were ready to begin our attack.
'Ah, ze terrible scenes of War. Ze mushrooms fired valiantly at ze
corn so 'igh above, and ze ants charged and charged again, carrying us
to ze very top even as zey were attacked by 'orrible birds. It was a long
campaign in ze wind and rain, but by Summer I could look
out over a sea of soldiers, swaying in ze wheat as eet turned to gold. We
'ad taken ze 'ole field.
'Now we waited, patient as ze wheat ripened under ze sun. Finally, ze
great day arrived. Ze living came to cut ze wheat. We were 'idden,

disguised
as ears of corn zat
'ad gone black in ze
sun. Naturally, we were
'arvested, zen made into flour,
zen finally baked in bread and eaten.
Oh ze joy!

'We went to work immediately.

Zere were people running wild in ze streets and talking
to thin air, and dancing and lunacy of all sorts.
And still ze people continued to eat, thinking eet was ze work
of magic, never suspecting us.
'Ow we laughed as persons were taken away and 'anged for witch
craft, while uzzers 'oo 'ad eaten more of us convulsed and found
zat zeir arms and legs no longer worked.
'Eventually, zey fell off completely and ze persons died
wailing een pain. Ahhh, it was ze best of times.
'In ze end everyone was killed, and no one lived zere ever
again. It was a triumph for me, ze brilliant Lord Ergot.
A battle zat will never be forgotten.'
Field Marshal Ergot fell into a trance
of happy remembrance for a moment and then said, '
'Zo, I shall 'elp you plan ze campaign to keel zis
person 'oo we all 'ate so much. And zen yoo and
I weel make ze world tremble my friend.'

'Yes My Lord
Ergot, I replied
'I promise.

Scientific (Latin) Name: Strychnos nux-vomica
Other Names: Poison Nut, Semen Strychnos, Quaker Buttons

Appearance: The seeds that contain the poison grow on a small
tree that has a crooked, thick trunk and even grey bark. It has
oval, shiny leaves and little white-green flowers which are
funnel-shaped and have a nasty smell.
The seeds are found within soft, orange-coloured fruit and are
flat and round with a sheen.

Symptoms: Breathing becomes deep and fast and the heart-rate is
slowed while all the senses become sharper.
This is followed by violent convulsions
and a massive rise in blood pressure.

Medicinal Uses: Tiny doses of Strychnine were
once commonly used in tonics, for the
stimulating effect the poison has on the body,
but now it is used only as a poison.

4.

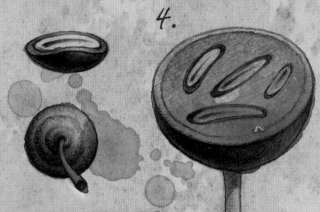

Nux Vomica

1.

2.

3.

1. Leaves: Oval, grooved
   and glossy green.
2. Flowers: Small and trumpet-shaped.
3. Fruits: Squashy and orange.
4. Seeds: Flat, shiny and very poisonous.

I found **Nux Vomica** in a small glasshouse. Before I could say anything, she began to talk in a stern voice that demanded obedience. 'You will use the seeds I will give you to make Strychnine and you will poison this apothecary person. If you fail to do so, I will be greatly displeased. Do you wish me to be displeased, Weed?

Would you like to be punished?'

It must have been only a branch, but it seemed that she swished a cane as though longing to whip me with it. Quickly I said, 'No, Miss, umm...

'Those who satisfy are allowed to call me Strict Nina, or Mistress Strict. For now you will call me Mistress, but when the vile man is dead we shall see. If, on the other hand, you fail me,' she said with another swish of her cane, 'you will find that I like to inflict exquisite pain, young Weed.'

'Yes Mistress, but how should Strychnine be used?' As I asked the question, it was as if something broke inside me. I was to be a killer, and I laughed with joy. Now I could truly be at one with my friends, my wonderful, wicked friends.

'A good question, you will be an excellent pupil, Weed.' I grinned and Mistress Strict continued. 'My poison is potent and can be used in many ways. For example, there was once a young queen. She had a sister who plotted to take over the throne and through her spies the queen learned of her sister's scheme to murder her. A most vulgar death it was to be, involving swords or knives or spoons or some such cutlery.

'The night before the deed was to be committed, the queen arranged a dance and ordered everyone to attend. While her sister bathed, the queen stole into her rooms and soaked her sister's corsets with water in which Strychnine had been dissolved, then she put the undergarments before the fire to dry.

'Of course, the maid had no idea what had been done and laced the princess tightly into her corset before the ball. Dressed in her finery and thinking that the next day the queen would be dead, she went down to the great hall and danced with delight all night long, faster and faster as the music became wild. As she danced her sweat dissolved the Strychnine in her bodice and it entered her body through the tiny pores in her skin. 'By then it was already too late for her.'

'What happened next?' I asked eagerly.

'She retired to her room feeling unwell, and within a few hours she was stiff and thrashing on the bed. It was most painful for her. By morning she was dead.'

Mistress Strict smiled for the first time. 'Stiff and thrashing, Weed. It is a fine sight.' I clapped my hands. 'Mistress, I cannot wait to begin.' 'Good, you must not disappoint me.' She swished her cane one more time and then asked me in a hopeful voice... 'Before you go, would you like a little taste of agony?'

It is done.

The master came down to breakfast to find everything
prepared. Eggs and sausages glistened on his plate and
tea with rum in it was steaming in the pot.

In the grate a fire burned cheerfully.
With a grunt he sat and ate, like a pig at the trough,
unaware that throughout the forest, the poisons that he had cultivated for so long
were singing songs of victory and joy.
The potion I had toiled over during the night was in everything that touched his lips.

For two hours little happened, though the master complained of a dry,
sore throat in a hoarse voice as we worked. He seemed a little confused.
That must be Belladonna and the Lords and Ladies, I thought.
For a while there was nothing else.

I was beginning to think that something must have gone wrong,
when the master clutched at his stomach and

ran to the outhouse.

I followed and listened at the door. At first, I just heard deep groans and gasps, and the
sound of his trousers being hastily taken down. Then came agonized gurgles of heaving sickness
and the splashes of fountains of vomit hitting the walls and floor. At the same time, there were
great trumpet noises of wet farting and more splattering on the floor. Wafts of the most vile
smells came through the little apple-shaped hole that was cut in the door. A breeze tickled the tops of
the trees that surround the cottage, and in the garden I heard the plants beginning to cheer. Trying to make
my voice sound concerned while smiling broadly, I asked, 'Master, are
you unwell? Was it the sausages do you think? They were fresh yesterday.'
His voice was faint now as he replied, 'Do you think I am stupid, boy? Do you not think that I of all people would
not know that I have been poisoned? I am dying, as that girl in the woods died.' My heart froze as the privy
door flew open. The apothecary tottered there for a second, towering huge and wicked
over me, with the fire of absolute hatred and fury in his eyes. Then he
fell to his knees as great convulsions racked
his body.

Covered in his own filth and sick, he
began to crawl towards me, a murderous scowl
on his face and his panting voice a husky growl.
'Yes, I know about Marigold,' he panted.
'And I know there is no Belladonna
anywhere around here but in the
garden. You gave it to her, you nasty
little vermin.' Another
convulsion gripped him.
'Belladonna,
Lords and Ladies, and...
ahh, Ricin. Am I right?'
I nodded and stepped back
from him as he reached up to
me from his knees, his hands now
claws that would rip me apart.
I was not afraid. In my mind,
flowers blossomed and berries fruited.
Branches and stems twisted around my
thoughts. I was calm.
From the forest I heard voices:

'Ha Ha ha HEEE, AHHHH, SPASM!'
and, 'I say, the boy's doing rather well m'dear,
haw haw.' Then the apothecary's face froze and his
hand became a rigid claw, his entire body now stiff
and unmoving. 'Hemlock and Strychnine too,' he
managed to whisper. Beads of sweat began to gather on
his brow. 'And Nicotiana... you have learned well.'
For a while, he was unable to move and I thought
that it must be the end. Then the apothecary began
to tremble, slightly at first, but soon with great
racking shudders.
His eyes were wide and glistening now and
he started talking again, gibbering in a croaking
voice that he could fly like a bee, and making
buzzing noises.
It could have been Ergot
or Belladonna or Henbane,
or all three of them.

—Suddenly, he stood and began to move, at once stiffly, but vibrating like a tuning fork. The flies buzzing around him became more excited. He got as far as the workshop then toppled against a bench, shattering tubes and bottles. Rivers of vomit mixed with blood streamed from his mouth. Now he began thrashing like a tree in a gale, this way and that, with clutching, bloodless fingers. Ergot was withering his limbs already. I fetched my journal from my room and made some sketches and notes as he died, his evil old face contorted with pain and his body twisted like an old root. In the ruins of his laboratory, smashed bottles dripped and foul-smelling potions ran into one another. Finally, his eyes rolled up into his head and all movement stopped.

My potion had finished its work and the disgusting old master could hurt no-one any more. A cloud of flies settled on his face.

When I had finished my drawing, I collected my belongings together and took a great bag of coins the apothecary had hidden in his rooms. Then I went down to the garden for the very last time.

As I entered, the plants were quiet and it seemed they all bowed to me. I said goodbye to each one in turn and collected samples and clippings, carefully storing them in my bag. Finally, I stood before Belladonna.

'What will you do now?' she said. I grinned, and my hair twisted around my face as if it were alive as I bent over to whisper to her. 'I will do whatever I like,' I said.

'I am the Great Weed.'

All of the characters and storylines in this work are
fictitious. None of the information enclosed is for
practical use and is in no way intended as a guide.
Plant poisons can be dangerous when used incorrectly
and should only be handled by a qualified professional.
The moral of The Poison Diaries is that plants can kill.

First published in the United Kingdom
in 2006 by Pavilion
151 Freston Road
London
W10 6TH

An imprint of Anova Books Company Ltd

Published in North America by Abrams, an imprint of
Harry N. Abrams, Inc.

Library of Congress Control Number: 2006934708
ISBN 13: 978-0-8109-9314-3
ISBN 10: 0-8109-9314-7

10 9 8 7 6 5 4 3 2 1

Reproduction by Mission Productions Ltd, Hong Kong
Printed and bound by SNP Leefung Printing Co Ltd, China

HNA
harry n. abrams, inc.
a subsidiary of La Martinière Groupe

115 West 18th Street
New York, NY 10011
www.hnabooks.com